Water Sports

Carmel Reilly

Contents

What Are Water Sports?

Every year, lots of children and their families play or watch water sports.

Water sports are played at swimming pools, rivers, lakes or in the sea.

Some of these sports are swimming, surfing, water-skiing, sailing, windsurfing and water polo.

Swimming

Most children love to swim.

Some of them like to swim in the sea,

or in a lake or river.

Others like to go to a swimming pool.

Swimming is a good way to keep fit.

Some children are in swimming teams.
They practise every day
to get ready for swimming races.

Surfing

Surfing is a beach sport.
Surfers **paddle** out to sea on their surfboards.
Then, they let the waves
carry them back to the beach.

Surfers have to practise a lot
to become good at their sport.
They must be fit and strong
to paddle over waves
and to stand up on their surfboards.

Surfers have to be very good swimmers, too.

Water-skiing

The best place to water-ski is on a lake,
where the water is flat, without waves.

The water-skier holds on to a long rope
that is tied behind a boat.
The **skier** is pulled very fast
across the water.

Most water-skiers wear skis,
but a lot of children ride on boards.

Some water-skiers like to do tricks
while they are skiing.
Many of them can jump or turn around
as they move along.

Sailing

Some children go sailing with their parents.
Big children can help to sail the boat.
Young children often just watch and have fun.

Some people like to race sailing boats.
Others like to take long trips across the sea.

Most sailing boats have cabins.
People can eat and sleep in cabins
when they go away on sailing trips.

Some families live on sailing boats all the time.

Windsurfing

Some older children ride on surfboards with sails.
This sport is called windsurfing.
When the wind blows into the sails,
the boards go faster and faster across the water.

It takes lots of practice
to become a good **windsurfer**.

Some people can make their boards
move very quickly across the waves.
They can even make their boards
jump into the air.

Water Polo

Water polo is a team sport.
It is played in a swimming pool, with a ball.
There is a goal net at each end of the pool.

Each team has six players and a **goalkeeper**.
The players try to get the ball
into their goal net.
The goalkeeper tries to stop
the other team from getting a goal.

Water sports are lots of fun.
Children need to know how to swim,
and how to keep themselves safe at all times.

Glossary

goalkeeper   someone who tries to stop
the other team from getting a goal

paddle   to move through the water,
sometimes on top of a surfboard

skier   a person on skis who is pulled
across the water by boat

windsurfer   a person who uses the wind
to ride on a surfboard with a sail